THE BALLAD OF
THE WHITE HORSE
G. K. CHESTERTON

THE BALLAD OF THE WHITE HORSE

BY

G. K. CHESTERTON

"I SAY, AS DO ALL CHRISTIAN MEN, THAT IT IS A DIVINE
PURPOSE THAT RULES, AND NOT FATE."
KING ALFRED'S ADDITION TO "BOETHIUS"

METHUEN & CO. LTD.
36 ESSEX STREET W.C.
LONDON

PREFATORY NOTE

THIS ballad needs no historical notes, for the simple reason that it does not profess to be historical. All of it that is not frankly fictitious, as in any prose romance about the past, is meant to emphasize tradition rather than history. King Alfred is not a legend in the sense that King Arthur may be a legend; that is, in the sense that he may possibly be a lie. But King Alfred is a legend in this broader and more human sense, that the legends are the most important things about him.

The cult of Alfred was a popular cult, from the darkness of the ninth century to the deepening twilight of the twentieth. It is

BALLAD OF THE WHITE HORSE

wholly as a popular legend that I deal with him here. I write as one ignorant of everything, except that I have found the legend of a King of Wessex still alive in the land. I will give three curt cases of what I mean. A tradition connects the ultimate victory of Alfred with the valley in Berkshire called the Vale of the White Horse. I have seen doubts of the tradition, which may be valid doubts. I do not know when or where the story started; it is enough that it started somewhere and ended with me; for I only seek to write upon a hearsay, as the old balladists did. For the second case, there is a popular tale that Alfred played the harp and sang in the Danish camp; I select it because it is a popular tale, at whatever time it arose. For the third case, there is a popular tale that Alfred came in contact with a woman and cakes: I select it because it is a popular tale, because it is a vulgar one. It has been disputed by grave historians, who were, I think.

a little too grave to be good judges of it. The two chief charges against the story are, that it was first recorded long after Alfred's death, and that (as Mr. Oman urges) Alfred never really wandered all alone without any thanes or soldiers. Both these objections might possibly be met. It has taken us nearly as long to learn the whole truth about Byron, and perhaps longer to learn the whole truth about Pepys, than elapsed between Alfred and the first writing of such tales. And as for the other objection, do the historians really think that Alfred after Wilton, or Napoleon after Leipsic, never walked about in a wood by himself for the matter of an hour or two? Ten minutes might be made sufficient for the essence of the story. But I am not concerned to prove the truth of these popular traditions. It is enough for me to maintain two things: that they are popular traditions; and that without these popular traditions we should have

BALLAD OF THE WHITE HORSE

bothered about Alfred about as much as we bother about Eadwig.

One other consideration needs a note, Alfred has come down to us in the best way (that is by national legends) solely for the same reason as Arthur and Roland and the other giants of that darkness, because he fought for the Christian civilization against the heathen nihilism. But since this work was really done by generation after generation, by the Romans before they withdrew, and by the Britons while they remained, I have summarised this first crusade in a triple symbol, and given to a fictitious Roman, Celt, and Saxon, a part in the glory of Ethandune, I fancy that in fact Alfred's Wessex was of very mixed bloods : but in any case, it is the chief value of legend to mix up the centuries while preserving the sentiment ; to see all ages in a sort of splendid foreshortening. That is the use of tradition : it telescopes history. G. K. C.

CONTENTS

	PAGE
DEDICATION	xiii

BOOK I
THE VISION OF THE KING 1

BOOK II
THE GATHERING OF THE CHIEFS . . . 21

BOOK III
THE HARP OF ALFRED 41

BOOK IV
THE WOMAN IN THE FOREST 67

BOOK V
ETHANDUNE: THE FIRST STROKE . . . 89

BOOK VI
ETHANDUNE: THE SLAYING OF THE CHIEFS . 109

BOOK VII
ETHANDUNE: THE LAST CHARGE . . . 131

BOOK VIII
THE SCOURING OF THE HORSE . . . 157

TO
MY VIFE
DEDICATION

great limbs gone to chaos,

A great face turned to night Why bend above a shapeless shroud Seeking in such archaic cloud Sight of strong lords and light ?

Where seven sunken Enfflands

Lie buried one by one, Why should one idle spade, I wonder, Shake up the dust of thanes like thunder

To smoke and choke the sun ?

BALLAD OF THE WHITE HORSE

In cloud of clay so cast to heaven What shape shall man discern ?

These lords may light the mystery

Of mastery or victory,

And these ride high in history, But these shall not return.

Gored on the Norman gonfalon

The Golden Dragon died ; We shall not wake with ballad strings The good time of the smaller things, We shall not see the holy kings

Ride down by Severn side.

Stiff, strange, and quaintly coloured

As the broidery of Bayeux The England of that dawn remains, And this of Alfred and the Danes Seems like the tales a whole tribe feigns,

Too English to be true.

Of a good king on an island

That ruled once on a time ; And as he walked by an apple tree There came green devils out of the sea With sea-plants trailing heavily

And tracks of opal slime.

Yet Alfred is no fairy tale;

His days as our days ran, He also looked forth for an hour On peopled plains and skies that lower, From those few windows in the tower

That is the head of a man.

But who shall look from Alfred's hood

Or breathe his breath alive ? His century like a small dark cloud Drifts far; it is an eyeless crowd, Where the tortured trumpets scream aloud

And the dense arrows drive.

BALLAD OF THE WHITE HORSE

Lady, by one light only

We look from Alfred's eyes, We know he saw athwart the wreck The sign that hangs about your neck, Where One more than Melchizedek

Is dead and never dies.

Therefore I bring these rhymes to you,

Who brought the cross to me. Since on you flaming without flaw I saw the sign that Guthrum saw When he let break his ships of awe,

And laid peace on the sea.

Do you remember when we went
Under a dragon moon, And 'mid volcanic tints of night Walked where they fought the unknown fight And saw black trees on the battle-height,
Black thorn on Ethandune ?
And I thought, " I will go with you,
As man with God has gone, And wander with a wandering star. The wandering heart of things that are. The fiery cross of love and war
That like yourself, goes on."
O go you onward; where you are
Shall honour and laughter be, Past purple forest and pearled foam, God's winged pavilion free to roam. Your face, that is a wandering home,
A flying home for me.
Ride through the silent earthquake lands.
Wide as a waste is wide. Across these days like deserts, when Pride and a little scratching pen Have dried and split the hearts of men,
Heart of the heroes, ride.

BALLAD OF THE WHITE HORSE

Up through an empty house of stars,
Being what heart you are, Up the inhuman steeps of space As on a staircase go in grace. Carrying the firelight on your face
Beyond the loneliest star.
Take these; in memory of the hour
We strayed a space from home And saw the smoke-hued hamlets, quaint With Westland king and Westland saint, And watched the western glory faint Along the road to Frome.
G. K. C.
THE BALLAD OF THE WHITE HORSE
BOOK I
THE VISION OF THE KING
T)EFORE the gods that made the gods
Had seen their sunrise pass, The White Horse of the White Horse Vale Was cut out of the grass.
Before the gods that made the gods
Had drunk at dawn their fill, The AVhite Horse of the White Horse Vale
Was hoary on the hill.
BALLAD OF THE WHITE HORSE
Age beyond age on British land,
ons on aeons gone, Was peace and war in western hills,
And the White Horse looked on.
For the White Horse knew England
When there was none to know; He saw the first oar break or bend, He saw heaven fall and the world end, O God, how long ago.
For the end of the world was long ago-
And all we dwell to-day As children of some second birth. Like a strange people left on earth
After a judgment day.

For the end of the world was long ago, When the ends of the world waxed free,
When Rome was sunk in a waste of slaves, And the sun drowned in the sea.
When Caesar's sun fell out of the sky And whoso hearkened right
Could only hear the plunging Of the nations in the nisrht.
When the ends of the earth came marchins: in
To torch and cresset gleam, And the roads of the world that lead to
Rome Were filled with faces that moved like foam,
Like faces in a dream.

BALLAD OF THE WHITE HORSE

And men rode out of the eastern lands,
Broad river and burning plain; Trees that are Titan flowers to see, And tiger skies, striped horribly,
With tints of tropic rain.
Where Ind's enamelled peaks arise
Around that inmost one, Where ancient eagles on its brink, Vast as archangels, gather and drink
The sacrament of the sun.
And men brake out of the northern lands.
Enormous lands alone, Where a spell is laid upon life and lust And the rain is changed to a silver dust
And the sea to a great green stone.
And a Shape that moveth murkily
In mirrors of ice and night, Hath blanched with fear all beasts and birds, As death and a shock of evil words
Blast a man's hair with white.
And the cry of the palms and the purple moons, Or the cry of the frost and foam,
Swept ever around an inmost place.
And the din of distant race on race Cried and replied round Rome,
And there was death on the Emperor And night upon the Pope;
And Alfred, hiding in deep grass, Hardened his heart with hope.

BALLAD OF THE WHITE HORSE

A sea-folk blinder than the sea
Broke all about his land, But Alfred up against them bare And gripped the ground and grasped the air,
Staggered, and strove to stand.
He bent them back with spear and spade,
With desperate dyke and wall, With foemen leaning on his shield And roaring on him when he reeled ;
And no help came at all.
He broke them with a broken sword
A little towards the sea. And for one hour of panting peace. Ringed with a roar that would not cease. With golden crown and girded fleece
Made laws under a tree.

THE VISION OF THE KING

The Northmen came about our land
A Christless chivalry: Who knew not of the arch or pen, Great, beautiful half-witted men
From the sunrise and the sea.

Misshapen ships stood on the deep
Full of strange gold and fire, And hairy men, as huge as sin, With horned heads, came wading in
Through the long, low sea-mire.
Our towns were shaken of tall kings
With scarlet beards like blood; The world turned empty where they trod. They took the kindly cross of God And cut it up for wood.

BALLAD OF THE WHITE HORSE

Their souls were drifting as the sea, And all good towns and lands
They only saw with heavy eyes, And broke with heavy hands.
Their gods were sadder than the sea,
Gods of a wandering will. Who cried for blood like beasts at night.
Sadly, from hill to hill.
They seemed as trees walking the earth,
As witless and as tall, Yet they took hold upon the heavens
And no help came at all.
They bred like birds in English woods.
They rooted like the rose. When Alfred came to Athelney
To hide him from their bows.

THE VISION OF THE KING

There was not English armour left,
Nor any English thing, When Alfred came to Athelney
To be an English king.
For earthquake swallowing earthcjuake
Uprent the Wessex tree; The whirlpool of the pagan sway Had swirled his sires as sticks away
When a flood smites the sea.
And the great kings of Wessex
Wearied and sank in gore, And even their ghosts in that great stress Grew greyer and greyer, less and less. With the lords that died in Lyonesse
And the king that comes no more.

BALLAD OF THE WHITE HORSE

And the God of the Golden Dragon Was dumb upon his throne,
And the lord of the Golden Dragon Ran in the woods alone.
And if ever he climbed the crest of luck
And set the flag before, Returning as a wheel returns. Came ruin and the rain that burns.
And all began once more.
And naught was left Kin"; Alfred But shameful tears of rage,
In the island in the river In the end of all his age.

THE VISION OF THE KING

In the island in the river
He was broken to his knee ; And he read, writ with an iron pen, That God had wearied of Wessex men And given their country, field and fen,
To the devils of the sea.
And he saw in a little picture.
Tiny and far away, His mother sitting in Egbert's hall. And a book she showed him, very small, Where a sapphire Mary sat in stall

With a golden Christ at play.

It was wrought in the monk's slow manner, From silver and sanguine shell,

Where the scenes are little and terrible. Keyholes of heaven and hell.

BALLAD OF THE WHITE HORSE

In the river island of Athelney,

With the river running past, In colours of such simple creed All things sprang at him, sun and weed, Till the grass grew to be grass indeed

And the tree was a tree at last.

Fearfully plain the flowers grew, Like the child's book to read.

Or like a friend's face seen in a glass ;

He looked; and there Our Lady was,

She stood and stroked the tall live grass As a man strokes his steed.

Her face was like an open word

When brave men speak and choose.

The very colours of her coat Were better than good news.

THE VISION OF THE KING

She spoke not, nor turned not,

Nor any sign she cast, Only she stood up straight and free, Between the flowers in Athehiey,

And the river running past.

One dim ancestral jewel hung

On his ruined armour grey, He rent and cast it at her feet: Where, after centuries, with slow feet. Men came from hall and school and street

And found it where it lay.

" Mother of God," the wanderer said,

" I am but a common king. Nor will I ask what saints may ask,

To see a'jsecret thing.

BALLAD OF THE WHITE HORSE

" The gates of heaven are fearful gates

Worse than the gates of hell; Not I would break the splendours barred Or seek to know the thing they guard,

Which is too good to tell.

" But for this earth most pitiful,

This little land I know, If that which is for ever is, Or if our hearts shall break with bliss,

Seeing the stranger go ?

" When our last bow is broken, Queen,

And our last javelin cast, Under some sad, green evening sky, Holding a ruined cross on high, Under warm westland grass to lie,

Shall we come home at last ? "

THE VISION OF THE KING

And a voice came human but high up,

Like a cottage climbed among The clouds; or a serf of hut and croft That sits by his hovel fire as oft, But hears on his old bare roof aloft

A belfry burst in song.

" The gates of heaven are lightly locked,

We do not guard our gain, The heaviest hind may easily Come silently and suddenly

Upon me in a lane,

" And any little maid that walks

In good thoughts apart. May break the guard of the Three Kings And see the dear and dreadful things

I hid within my heart.

BALLAD OF THE WHITE HORSE

" The meanest man in grey fields gone

Behind the set of sun, Heareth between star and other star, Through the door of the darkness fallen ajar, The council, eldest of things that are.

The talk of the Three in One.

" The gates of heaven are lightly locked,

We do not guard our gold, Men may uproot where worlds begin. Or read the name of the nameless sin ; But if he fail or if he win

To no good man is told.

" The men of the East may spell the stars. And times and triumphs mark.

But the men signed of the cross of Christ Go gaily in the dark.

THE VISION OF THE KING

" The men of the East may search the scrolls

For sure fates and fame, But the men that drink the blood of God

Go singing to their shame.

" The wise men know what wicked things

Are written on the sky, They trim sad lamps, they touch sad strings, Hearing the heavy purple wings. Where the forgotten seraph kings

Still plot how God shall die.

" The wise men know all evil things

Under the twisted trees. Where the perverse in pleasure pine And men are weary of green wine

And sick of crimson seas.

BALLAD OF THE WHITE HORSE

" But you and all the kind of Christ

Are ignorant and brave, And you have wars you hardly win

And souls you hardly save.

" I tell you naught for your comfort, Yea, naught for your desire,

Save that the sky grows darker yet And the sea rises higher.

" Night shall be thrice night over you.

And heaven an iron cope. Do you have joy without a cause.

Yea, faith without a hope ? "

Even as she spoke she was not.

Nor any word said he, He only heard, still as he stood

THE VISION OF THE KING

Under the old nighfs nodding hood, The sea-folk breaking down the wood Like a high tide from sea.

He only heard the heathen men,

Whose eyes are blue and bleak, Singing about some cruel thing Done by a great and smiling king In daylight on a deck.

He only heard the heathen men, Whose eyes are blue and blind. Singing what shameful things are done Between the sunlit sea and the sun When the land is left behind.

BOOK II

THE GATHERING OF THE CHIEFS

TTP across windy wastes and up
Went Alfred over the shaws, Shaken of the joy of giants, The joy without a cause.
In the slopes away to the western bays, Where blows not ever a tree,
He washed his soul in the west wind And his body in the sea.

22 BALLAD OF THE WHITE HORSE

And he set to rhyme his ale-measures,
And he sang aloud his laws, Because of the joy of the giants,
The joy without a cause.
For the King went gathering Wessex men,
As grain out of the chaff, The few that were alive to die. Laughing, as littered skulls that lie After lost battles turn to the sky
An everlasting laugh.
The King went gathering Christian men,
As wheat out of the husk ; Eldred, the Franklin by the sea. And Mark, the man from Italy, And Golan of the Sacred Tree,
From the old tribe on Usk.

THE GATHERING OF THE CHIEFS

The rook croaked homeward heavily,
The west was clear and warm, The smoke of evening food and ease Rose like a blue tree in the trees
When he came to Eldred's farm.
But Eldred*'s farm was fallen awry,
Like an old cripple's bones, And Eldred's tools were red with rust, And on his well was a green crust, And purple thistles upward thrust,
Between the kitchen stones.
But smoke of some good feasting
Went upwards evermore, And Eldred's doors stood wide apart For loitering foot or labouring cart. And Eldred's great and foolish heart
Stood open like his door.

BALLAD OF THE WHITE HORSE

A mighty man was Eldred,
A bulk for casks to fill, His face a dreaming furnace,
His body a walking hill.
In the old wars of Wessex
His sword had sunken deep, But all his friends, he sighed and said, Were broken about Ethelred ; And between the deep drink and the dead
He had fallen upon sleep.
" Come not to me, King Alfred,
Save always for the ale ; Why should my harmless hinds be slain Because the chiefs cry once again. As in all fights, that we shall gain,
And in all fights we fail ?

THE GATHERING OF THE CHIEFS

" Your scalds still thunder and prophesy
That crown that never comes; Friend, I will watch the certain things, Swine, and slow moons like silver rings. And the ripening of the plums."
And Alfred answered, drinking.

And gravely, without blame, " Nor bear I boast of scald or king. The thing I bear is a lesser thing,

But comes in a better name.

" Out of the mouth of the Mother of God,

More than the doors of doom, I call the muster of Wessex men From grassy hamlet or ditch or den, To break and be broken, God knows when,

But I have seen for whom.

BALLAD OF THE WHITE HORSE

" Out of the mouth of the Mother of God

Like a little word come I; For I go gathering Christian men From sunken paving and ford and fen, To die in a battle, God knows when,

By God, but I know why.

" And this is the word of Mary,

The word of the worWs desire : ' No more of comfort shall ye get. Save that tlie sky grows darker yet And the sea rises higher.'"

Then silence sank. And slowly

Arose the sea-land lord. Like some vast beast for mystery, He filled the room and porch and sky. And from a cobwebbed nail on high

LTnhooked his heavy sword.

THE GATHERING OF THE CHIEFS

Up on the shrill sea-downs and up

Went Alfred all alone, Turning but once e'er the door was shut, Shouting to Eldred over his butt. That he bring all spears to the woodman's hut

Hewn under Egbert's Stone.

And he turned his back and broke the fern,

And fought the moths of dusk, And went on his way for other friends. Friends fallen of all the wide world's ends, From Rome that wrath and pardon sends

And the grey tribes on Usk.

He saw gigantic tracks of death

And many a shape of doom. Good steadings to grey ashes gone And a monk's house white like a skeleton

In the green crypt of the combe.

BALLAD OF THE WHITE HORSE

And in many a Roman villa

Earth and her ivies eat, Saw coloured pavements sink and fade In flowers, and the windy colonnade

Like the spectre of a street.

But the cold stars clustered

Among the cold pines Ere he was half on his pilgrimage

Over the western lines.

And the white dawn widened

Ere he came to the last pine, Where Mark, the man from Italy,

Still made the Christian sign.

The long farm lay on the large hill-side, Flat like a painted plan.

THE GATHERING OF THE CHIEFS

And by the side the low white house, Where dwelt the southland man.

A bronzed man, with a bird's bright eye.

And a strong bird's beak and brow, His skin was brown like buried gold. And of certain of his sires was told That they came in the shining ship of old, With Caesar in the prow.

His fruit trees stood like soldiers

Drilled in a straight line, His strange, stiff olives did not fail, And all the kings of the earth drank ale,

But he drank wine.

Wide over wasted British plains Stood never an arch or dome. Only the trees to toss and reel,

BALLAD OF THE WHITE HORSE

The tribes to bicker, the beasts to squeal; But the eyes in his head were strong like steel, And his soul remembered Rome.

Then Alfred of the lonely spear

Lifted his lion head ; And fronted with the Italian's eye, Asking him of his whence and why.

King Alfred stood and said:

" I am that oft-defeated King,

Whose failure fills the land, Who fled before the Danes of old, Who chaffered with the Danes with gold, Who now upon the Wessex wold

Hardly has feet to stand.

THE GATHERING OF THE CHIEFS

"But out of the mouth of the Mother of God

I have seen the truth like fire, This—that the sky grows darker yet

And the sea rises higher."

Long looked the Roman on the land;

The trees as golden crowns Blazed, drenched with dawn and dew-em-pearled, While faintlier coloured, freshlier curled, The clouds from underneath the world

Stood up over the downs.

" These vines be ropes that drag me hard,"

He said. " I go not far; Where would you meet ? For you must hold

BALLAD OF THE WHITE HORSE

Half Wiltshire and the White Horse wold. And the Thames bank to Owsenfold, If Wessex goes to war.

" Guthrum sits strong on either bank

And you must press his lines Inwards, and eastward drive him down ; I doubt if you shall take the crown Till you have taken London town.

For me, I have the vines.""

" If each man on the Judgment Day

Meet God on a plain alone," Said Alfred, " I will speak for you As for myself, and call it true That you brought all fighting folk you knew

THE GATHERING OF THE CHIEFS

" Though I be in the dust ere then,

I know where you will be." And shouldering suddenly his spear He faded like some elfin fear, Where the tall pines ran up, tier on tier,

Tree overtoppling tree.

He shouldered his spear at morning

And laughed to lay it on, But he leaned on his spear as on a staff. With might and little mood to laugh, Or ever he sighted chick or calf

Of Colan of Caerleon.
For the man dwelt in a lost land
Of boulders and broken men.
In a great grey cave far off to south
Where a thick green forest stopped the mouth,
Giving darkness in his den.

BALLAD OF THE WHITE HORSE

And the man was come like a shadow,
From the shadow of Druid trees, Where Usk, with mighty murmurings, Past Caerleon of the fallen kings, Goes out to ghostly seas.

Last of a race in ruin—
He spoke the speech of the Gaels; His kin were in holy Ireland,
Or up in the crags of Wales.
But his soul stood with his mother's folk,
That were of the rain-wrapped isle, Where Patrick and Brandan westerly Looked out at last on a landless sea And the sun's last smile.

THE GATHERING OF THE CHIEFS

His harp was carved and cunning. As the Celtic craftsman makes,
Graven all over with twisting shapes Like many headless snakes.
His harp was carved and cunning, His sword prompt and sharp,
And he was gay when he held the sword, Sad when he held the harp.
For the great Gaels of Ireland Are the men that God made mad.
For all their wars are merry, And all their songs are sad.
He kept the Roman order, He made the Christian sign;

BALLAD OF THE WHITE HORSE

But his eyes grew often blind and bright, And the sea that rose in the rocks at night Rose to his head Hke wine.

He made the sign of the cross of God,
He knew the Roman prayer, But he had unreason in his heart
Because of the gods that were.
Even they that walked on the high cliffs, High as the clouds were then,
Gods of unbearable beauty That broke the hearts of men.
And whether in seat or saddle,
Whether with frown or smile, Whether at feast or fight was he, He heard the noise of a nameless sea On an undiscovered isle.

THE GATHERING OF THE CHIEFS

Lifting the great green ivy
And the great spear lowering. One said, " I am Alfred of Wessex,
And I am a conquered king."
And the man of the cave made answer, And his eyes were stars of scorn,
" And better kings were conquered Or ever your sires were born.
" What goddess was your mother,
What fay your breed begot, That you should not die with Uther
And Arthur and Lancelot ?
" But when you win you brag and blow,
And when you lose you rail, Army of eastland yokels
Not strong enough to fail."

BALLAD OF THE WHITE HORSE

" I bring not boast or railing,""

Spake Alfred not in ire, " I bring of Our Lady a lesson set. This—that the sky grows darker yet

And the sea rises higher."

Then Colan of the Sacred Tree

Tossed his black mane on high, And cried, as rigidly he rose, " And if the sea and sky be foes, We will tame the sea and sky.""

Smiled Alfred, " Seek ye a fable More dizzy and more dread

Than all your mad barbarian tales Where the sky stands on its head ?

THE GATHERING OF THE CHIEFS

" A tale where a man looks down on the sky That has long looked down on him ;

A tale where a man can swallow a sea That might swallow the seraphim.

" Bring to the hut by Egbert's Stone

All bills and bows ye have." And Alfred strode off rapidly, And Colan of the Sacred Tree Went slowly to his cave.

BOOK III

THE HARP OF ALFRED

XN a tree that yawned and twisted

The King's few goods were flung, A mass-book mildewed, line by line, And weapons and a skin of wine, And an old harp imstrung.

By the yawning tree in the twilight

The King unbound his sword, Severed the harp of all his goods. And there in the cool and soundless woods

Sounded a single chord.

BALLAD OF THE WHITE HORSE

Then laughed; and watched the finches flash,

The sullen flies in swarm, And went unarmed over the hills,

With the harp upon his arm,

Until he came to the White Horse Vale

And saw across the plains, In the twilight high and far and fell, Like the fiery terraces of hell.

The camp fires of the Danes—

The fires of the Great Army

That was made of iron men, Whose lights of sacrilege and scorn Ran around England red as morn, Fires over Glastonbury Thorn

Fires out on Ely Fen.

And as he went by Vhite Horse Vale

He saw lie wan and wide The old horse graven, God knows when, By gods or beasts or what things then Walked a new world instead of men

And scrawled on the hill-side.

And when he came to White Horse Down

The great White Horse was grey, For it was ill scoured of the weed. And lichen and thorn could crawl and feed, Since the foes of settled house and creed Had swept old works away.

King Alfred gazed all sorrowful

At thistle and mosses grey. Till a rally of Danes with shield and bill

BALLAD OF THE WHITE HORSE

Rolled drunk over the dome of the hill, And, hearing of his harp and skill, They dragged him to their play.

And as they went through the high green grass They roared like the great green sea ;
But when they came to the red camp fire They were silent suddenly.

And as they went up the wastes away
They went reeling to and fro ; But when they came to the red camp fire
They stood all in a row.

For golden in the firelight,
With a smile carved on his lips, And a beard curled right cunningly. Was Guthrum of the Northern Sea,

The emperor of the ships
With three great earls King Guthrum
Went the rounds from fire to fire, With Harold, nephew of the King, And Ogier of the Stone and Sling, And Elf, whose gold lute had a string That sighed like all desire.

The Earls of the Great Army That no men born could tire.
Whose flames anear him or aloof
Took hold of towers or walls of proof,
Fire over Glastonbury roof And out on Ely, fire.
And Guthrum heard the soldiers' tale
And bade the stranger play ; Not harshly, but as one on high,

BALLAD OF THE WHITE HORSE

On a marble pillar in the sky, Who sees all folk that live and die— Pigmy and far away.
And Alfred, King of Wessex,

Looked on his conqueror— And his hands hardened ; but he played. And leaving all later hates unsaid, He sang of some old British raid

On the wild west march of yore.
He sang of war in the warm wet shires,

Where rain nor fruitage fails, Where England of the motley states Deepens like a garden to the gates In the purple walls of Wales.

He sang of the seas of savage heads
And the seas and seas of spears, Boiling all over OfFa's Dyke, What time a Wessex club could strike The kings of the mountaineers.

Till Harold laughed and snatched the harp,
The kinsman of the King, A big youth, beardless like a child, Whom the new wine of war sent wild,

Smote, and began to sing—
And he cried of the ships as eagles
That circle fiercely and fly, And sweep the seas and strike the towns
From Cyprus round to Skye.

BALLAD OF THE WHITE HORSE

How swiftly and with peril
They gather all good things, The high horns of the forest beasts,
Or the secret stones of kings.

" For Rome was given to rule the world,
And gat of it little joy— But we, but we shall enjoy the world,
The whole huge world a toy.

" Great wine like blood from Burgundy, Cloaks like the clouds from Tyre,

And marble like solid moonlight, And gold like frozen fire.
" Smells that a man might swill in a cup, Stones that a man might eat.
And the great smooth women like ivory That the Turks sell in the street."
He sang the throne of the thief of the world, And the gods that love the thief;
And he yelled aloud at the cloister-yards, Where men go gathering grief.
" Well have you sung, O stranger,
Of death on the dyke in Wales, Your chief was a bracelet-giver ; But the red unbroken river Of a race runs not for ever,
But suddenly it fails.
" Doubtless your sires were sword-swingers
When they waded fresh from foam,
Before they were turned to women
By the god of the nails from Rome; 4
BALLAD OF THE WHITE HORSE
" But since you bent to the shaven men,
Who neither lust nor smite, Thunder of Thor, we hunt you,
A hare on the mountain height."
King Guthrum smiled a little, And said, " It is enough,
Nephew, let Elf retune the string;
A boy must needs like bellowing,
But the old ears of a careful king Are glad of songs less rough."
Blue-eyed was Elf the minstrel. With womanish hair and ring.
Yet heavy was his hand on sword. Though light upon the string.
And as he stirred the strings of the harp
To notes but four or five, The heart of each man moved in him
Like a babe buried alive.
And they felt the land of the folk-songs Spread southward of the Dane,
And they heard the good Rhine flowing In the heart of all Allemagne.
They felt the land of the folk-songs, Where the gifts hang on the tree,
Where the girls give ale at morning And the tears come easily.
The mighty people, womanlike. That have pleasure in their pain
As he sang of Balder beautiful. Whom the heavens loved in vain.
BALLAD OF THE WHITE HORSE
As he sang of Balder beautiful, Whom the heavens could not save,
Till the world was like a sea of tears And every soul a wave.
" There is always a thing forgotten
When all the world goes well; A thing forgotten, as long ago When the gods forgot the mistletoe, And soundless as an arrow of snow The arrow of anguish fell.
" The thing on the blind side of the heart, On the wrong side of the door,
The green plant groweth, menacing
Almighty lovers in the spring;
There is always a forgotten thing, And love is not secure.'^
And all that sat by the fire were sad,
Save Ogier, who was stern, And his eyes hardened, even to stones,
As he took the harp in turn ;
Earl Ogier of the Stone and Sling
Was odd to ear and sight. Old he was, but his locks were red. And jests were all the words

he said, Yet he was sad at board and bed

    And savage in the fight.

    " You sing of the young gods easily In the days when you are young;

    But I go smelling yew and sods.

    And I know there are gods behind the gods, Gods that are best unsung.

    BALLAD OF THE WHITE HORSE

    " And a man grows ugly for women, And a man grows dull with ale,

    Well if he find in his soul at last Fury, that does not fail.

    " The wrath of the gods behind the gods

    Who would rend all gods and men. Well if the old man's heart hath still Wheels sped of rage and roaring will, Like cataracts to break down and kill, Well for the old man then—

    " While there is one tall shrine to shake,

    Or one live man to rend ; For the wrath of the gods behind the gods

    Who are weary to make an end.

    " There lives one moment for a man

    When the door at his shoulder shakes, When the taut rope parts under the pull, And the barest branch is beautiful One moment, while it breaks.

    " So rides my soul upon the sea

    That drinks the howling ships. Though in black jest it bows and nods Under the moons with silver rods, I know it is roaring at the gods,

    Waiting the last eclipse.

    " And in the last eclipse the sea

    Shall stand up like a tower. Above all moons made dark and riven, Hold up its foaming head in heaven,

    And laugh, knowing its hour.

    BALLAD OF THE WHITE HORSE

    " And the high ones in the happy town

    Propped of the planets seven, Shall know a new light in the mind, A noise about them and behind, Shall hear an awful voice, and find

    Foam in the courts of heaven.

    " And you that sit by the fire are young. And true loves wait for you ;

    But the King and I grow old, grow old, And hate alone is true."

    And Guthrum shook his head but smiled,

    For he was a mighty clerk. And had read lines in the Latin books

    When all the north was dark.

    He said, " I am older than you, Ogier;

    Not all things would I rend. For whether life be bad or good

    It is best to abide the end."

    He took the great harp wearily,

    Even Guthrum of the Danes, With wide eyes bright as the one long day

    On the long polar plains.

    For he sang of a wheel returning. And the mire trod back to mire,

    And how red hells and golden heavens Are castles in the fire.

    " It is good to sit where the good tales go.

    To sit as our fathers sat; But the hour shall come after his youth. When a man shall know not tales but truth.

    And his heart fail thereat.

BALLAD OF THE WHITE HORSE

" When he shall read what is written
So plain in clouds and clods, When he shall hunger without hope
Even for evil sods.

" For this is a heavy matter, And the truth is cold to tell;
Do we not know, have we not heard.
The soul is like a lost bird, The body a broken shell.

" And a man hopes, being ignorant.
Till in white woods apart He finds at last the lost bird dead : And a man may still lift up his head But never more his heart.

" There comes no noise but weeping
Out of the ancient sky, And a tear is in the tiniest flower
Because the gods must die.

" The Httle brooks are very sweet,
Like a girl's ribbons curled. But the great sea is bitter
That washes all the world.

" Strong are the Roman roses, Or the free flowers of the heath.
But every flower, like a flower of the sea, Smelleth with the salt of death.

" And the heart of the locked battle
Is the happiest place for men ; When shrieking souls as shafts go by

BALLAD OF THE WHITE HORSE

And many have died and all may die; Though this word be a mystery, Death is most distant then.

" Death blazes bright above the cup,
And clear above the crown ; But in that dream of battle
We seem to tread it down.

" Wherefore I am a great king,
And waste the world in vain, Because man hath not other power, Save that in dealing death for dower. He may forget it for an hour
To remember it again."

And slowly his hands and thoughtfully Fell from the lifted lyre,
And the owls moaned from the mighty trees Till Alfred caught it to his knees And smote it as in ire.

He heaved the head of the harp on high And swept the framework baiTed,
And his stroke had all the rattle and spark Of horses flying hard.

" When God put man in a garden
He girt him with a sword, And sent him forth a free knight
That might betray his lord ;

" He brake Him and betrayed Him,
And fast and far he fell, Till you and I may stretch our necks
Aiid burn our beards in hell.

BALLAD OF THE WHITE HORSE

" But though I lie on the floor of the world,
With the seven sins for rods, I would rather fall with Adam
Than rise with all your gods.

" What have the strong gods given ?
Where have the glad gods led ? When Guthrum sits on a hero's throne

And asks if he is dead?
" Sirs, I am but a nameless man,
A rhymester without home, Yet since I come of the Wessex clay
And carry the cross of Rome,
" I will even answer the mighty earl That asked of Wessex men
Why they be meek and monkish folk, And bow to the White Lord's broken yoke; What sign have we save blood and smoke ? Here is my answer then.
" That on you is fallen the shadow,
And not upon the Name; That though we scatter and though we fly, And you hang over us like the sky, You are more tired of victory,
Than we are tired of shame.
" That though you hunt the Christian man
Like a hare on the hill-side. The hare has still more heart to run
Than you have heart to ride.

BALLAD OF THE WHITE HORSE

" That though all lances split on you,
All swords be heaved in vain, We have more lust again to lose
Than you to win again.
" Your lord sits high in the saddle,
A broken-hearted king, But our King Alfred, lost from fame. Fallen among foes or bonds of shame. In I know not what mean trade or name,
Has still some song to sing;
" Our monks go robed in rain and snow, But the heart of flame therein,
But you go clothed in feasts and flames, When all is ice within;
"Nor shall all iron dooms make dumb
Men wondering ceaselessly, If it be not better to fast for joy
Than feast for misery.
" Nor monkish order only
Slides down, as field to fen, All things achieved and chosen pass, As the White Horse fades in the grass. No work of Christian men.
" Ere the sad gods that made your gods
Saw their sad sunrise pass, The White Horse of the White Horse V^ale, That you have left to darken and fail,
Was cut out of the grass.
" Therefore your end is on you,
Is on you and your kings, Not for a fire in Ely fen, Not that your gods are nine or ten. But because it is only Christian men
Guard even heathen things,
" For our God hath blessed creation,
Calling it good. I know What spirit with whom you blindly band Hath blessed destruction with his hand; Yet by God's death the stars shall stand
And the small apples grow."
And the King, with harp on shoulder,
Stood up and ceased his song; And the owls moaned from the mighty trees.
And the Danes laughed loud and long.

BOOK IV

THE WOMAN IN THE FOREST

lHICK thunder of the snorting swine,
Enormous in the gloom, Rending among all roots that cling, And the wild horses whinnying. Were the nighfs noises when the King, Shouldering his harp, went home.

With eyes of owl and feet of fox,
Full of all thoughts he went; He marked the tilt of the pagan camp, The paling of pine, the sentries' tramp, And the one great stolen altar-lamp

Over Guthrum in his tent.

BALLAD OF THE WHITE HORSE

By scrub and thorn in Ethandune
That night the foe had lain ; Whence ran across the heather grey The old stones of a Roman way ; And in a wood not far away

The pale road split in twain.

He marked the wood and the cloven ways
With an old captain's eyes, And he thought how many a time had he Sought to see Doom he could not see; How ruin had come and victory,

And both were a surprise.

Even so he had watched and wondered

Under Ashdown from the plains; With Ethelred praying in his tent,

THE WOMAN IN THE FOREST

Till the white hawthorn swung and bent, As Alfred rushed his spears and rent The shield-wall of the Danes.

Even so he had watched and wondered, Knowing neither less nor more.

Till all his lords lay dying.

And axes on axes plying,

Flung him, and drove him Hying Like a pirate to the shore.

Wise he had been before defeat,

And wise before success; Wise in both hours, and ignorant,

Knowing neither more nor less.

As he went down to the river-hut He knew a night-shade scent,

BALLAD OF THE WHITE HORSE

Owls did as evil cherubs rise, With little wings and lantern eyes, As though he sank through the under-skies; But down and down he went.

As he went down to the river-hut

He went as one that fell; Seeing the high forest domes and spars, Dim green or torn with golden scars. As the proud look up at the evil stars.

In the red heavens of hell.

For he must meet by the river-hut

Them he had bidden to arm, Mark from the towers of Italy, And Colan of the Sacred Tree, And Eldred who beside the sea

Held heavily his farm.

THE WOMAN IN THE FOREST

The roof leaned gaping to the grass, As a monstrous mushroom lies;

Echoing and empty seemed the place;

But opened in a little space

A great grey woman with scarred face And strong and humbled eyes.

King Alfred was but a meagre man,

Bright eyed, but lean and pale: And swordless, with his harp and rags, He seemed a beggar, such as lags Looking for crusts and ale.

And the woman, with a woman's eyes

Of pity at once and ire. Said, when that she had glared a span, " There is a cake for any man

If he will watch the fire."

BALLAD OF THE WHITE HORSE

And Alfred, bowing heavily,

Sat down the fire to stir, And even as the woman pitied him

So did he pity her.

Saying, " O great heart in the night,

O best cast forth for worst, Twilight shall melt and morning stir. And no kind thing shall come to her. Till God shall turn the world over And all the last are first.

" And well may God with the serving-folk

Cast in His dreadful lot; Is not He too a servant.

And is not He forgot ?

THE WOMAN IN THE FOREST

" For was not God my gardener

And silent like a slave ; That opened oaks on the uplands

Or thicket in graveyard gave ?

" And was not God my armom-er, All patient and unpaid,

That sealed my skull as a helmet, And ribs for hauberk made ?

" Did not a great gi'ey servant

Of all my sires and me. Build this pavilion of the pines, And herd the fowls and fill the vines, And labour and pass and leave no signs

Save mercy and mystery ?

BALLAD OF THE WHITE HORSE

" For God is a great servant,

And rose before the day, From some primordial slumber torn ; But all we living later born Sleep on, and rise after the morn,

And the Lord has gone away.

" On things half sprung from sleeping.

All sleepy suns have shone, They stretch stiff' arms, the yawning trees. The beasts blink upon hands and knees, Man is awake and does and sees—

But Heaven has done and gone.

" For who shall guess the good riddle

Or speak of the Holiest, Save in faint figures and failing words. Who loves, yet laughs among the swords,

Labours, and is at rest ':!

"But some see God like Giithrum, Crowned, with a great beard curled,

But I see God like a good giant, That, labouring, lifts the world.

"Wherefore was God in Golgotha,

Slain as a serf is slain ; And hate He had of prince and peer. And love He had and made good cheer Of them that, like this woman here,

Go powerfully in pain.

" But in this grey morn of man's life Cometh sometime to the mind

A little light that leaps and flies, Like a star blown on the wind.

BALLAD OF THE WHITE HORSE

"A star of nowhere, a nameless star,
A light that spins and swirls. And cries that even in hedge and hill, Even on earth, it may go ill
At last with the evil earls.

"A dancing sparkle, a doubtful star.
On the waste wind whirled and driven ; But it seems to sing of a wilder worth, A time discrowned of doom and birth. And the kingdom of the poor on earth Come, as it is in heaven.

"But even though such days endure.
How shall it profit her ? Who shall go groaning to the grave. With many a meek and mighty slave. Field-breaker and fisher on the wave.
And woodman and waggoner.

THE WOMAN IN THE FOREST

"Bake ye the big world all again
A cake wth kinder leaven; Yet these are sorry evermore— Unless there be a little door,
A little door in heaven."
And as he wept for the woman
He let her business be, And like his royal oath and rash The good food fell upon the ash
And blackened instantly.
Screaming, the woman caught a cake
Yet burning from the bar, And struck him suddenly on the face,
Leaving a scarlet scar.
King Alfred stood up wordless, A man dead with surprise,

BALLAD OF THE WHITE HORSE

And torture stood and the evil things That are in the childish hearts of kino-s An instant in his eyes.
And even as he stood and stared
Drew round him in the dusk Those friends creeping from far-off farms, Marcus with all his slaves in arms, And the strange spears hung with ancient charms
Of Colan of the Usk.
With one whole farm marching afoot
The trampled road resounds, Farm-hands and farm-beasts Ijlundering by And jars of mead and stores of rye, Where Eldred strode above his high
And thunder-throated hounds.

THE WOMAN IN THE FOREST

And grey cattle and silver lowed
Against the unlifted morn, And straw clung to the spear-shafts tall, And a boy went before them all
Blowing a ram's horn.
As mocking such rude revelry,
The dim clan of the Gael Came like a bad king's burial-end, With dismal robes that drop and rend
And demon pipes that wail—
In long, outlandish garments.
Torn, though of antique worth, With Druid beards and Druid spears, As a resurrected race appears Out of an elder earth.

BALLAD OF THE WHITE HORSE

And though the King had called them forth

And knew them for his own, So still each eye stood like a gem, So spectral hung each broidered hem. Grey carven men he fancied them,

Hewn in an age of stone.

And the two wild peoples of the north

Stood fronting in the gloom. And heard and knew each in its mind The third great thunder on the wind. The living walls that hedge mankind.

The walking walls of Rome.

Mark's were the mixed tribes of the west.

Of many a hue and strain, Gurth, with rank hair like yellow grass. And the Cornish fisher, Gorlias,

THE WOMAN IN THE FOREST

And Halraer, come from his first mass, Lately baptized, a Dane.

But liiv.e one man in armour

Those hundreds trod the field. From red Arabia to the Tyne The earth had heard that marching-line, Since the cry on the hill Capitoline,

And the fall of the golden shield.

And the earth shook and the King stood still

Under the greenwood bough, And the smoking cake lay at his feet

And the blow was on his brow.

Then Alfred laughed out suddenly.

Like thunder in the spring.

Till shook aloud the lintel-beams,

BALLAD OF THE WHITE HORSE

And the squirrels stirred in dusty dreams, And the startled birds went up in streams, For the laughter of the King.

And the beasts of the earth and the birds looked down,

In a wild solemnity, On a stranger sight than a sylph or elf. On one man laughing at himself

Under the greenwood tree—

The giant laughter of Christian men

That roars through a thousand tales. Where greed is an ape and pride is an ass. And Jack's away with his master's lass. And the miser is banged with all his brass, The farmer with all his flails;

Tales that tumble and tales that trick,

Yet end not all in scorning— Of" kings and clowns in a merry plight, And the clock gone wrong and the world gone

right, That the mummers sing upon Christmas night

And Christmas Day in the morning.

" Now here is a good warrant,"

Cried Alfred, " by my sword; For he that is struck for an ill servant

Should be a kind lord.

" He that has been a servant

Knows more than priests and kings,

I\'7dut he that has been an ill servant, He knows all earthly things.

BALLAD OF THE AVHITE HORSE

" Pride flings frail palaces at the sky,

As a man flings up sand, But the firm feet of humility

Take hold of heavy land.

" Pride juggles with her toppling towers, They strike the sun and cease,

But the firm feet of humility They grip the ground like trees.

" He that hath failed in a little thing

Hath a sign upon the brow; And the Earls of the Great Army

Have no such seal to show.

" The red print on my forehead, Small flame for a red star,

THE WOMAN IN THE FOREST

In the van of tlie violent marching, then When the sky is torn of the trumpets ten. And the hands of the happy howling men Fling wide the gates of war.

" This blow that I return not

Ten times will I return On kings and earls of all degree, And armies wide as empires be Shall slide like landslips to the sea

If the red star burn.

" One man shall drive a hundred,

As the dead kings drave ; Before me rocking hosts be riven. And battering cohorts backwards driven. For I am the first king known of heaven

That has been struck like a slave.

BALLAD OF THE WHITE HORSE

" Up on the old white road, brothers,

Up on the Roman walls ! For this is the night of the drawing of swords, And the painted tower of the heathen hordes Leans to our hammers, fires and cords.

Leans a little and falls.

" Follow the star that lives and leaps.

Follow the sword that sings. For we go gathering heathen men, A terrible harvest, ten by ten, As the wrath of the last red autumn—then

When Christ reaps down the kings.

" Follow a light that leaps and spins,

Follow the fire unfurled ! For riseth up against realm and rod,

THE WOMAN IN THE FOREST

A thing forgotten, a thing downtrod. The last lost giant, even God, Is risen against the world."

Roaring they went o'er the Roman wall,

And roaring up the lane. Their torches tossed, a ladder of fire, Higher their hymn was heard and higher. More sweet for hate and for heart's desire. And up in the northern scrub and brier

They fell upon the Dane.

BOOK V

ETHANDUNE: THE FIRST STROKE

jr ING GUTHRUM was a dread king,

Like death out of tlie north ; Shrines without name or number He rent and rolled as lumber, From Chester to the Humber He drove his foemen forth.

The Roman villas heard him

In the valley of the Thames, Come over the hills roaring Above their roofs, and pouring On spire and stair and flooring

Brimstone and pitch and Hames.

BALLAD OF THE WHITE HORSE

Sheer o'er the great chalk uplands And the hill of the Horse went he,

Till high on Hampshire beacons He saw the southern sea.

High on the heights of Wessex

He saw the southern brine, And turned him to a conquered land. And where the nortliern thornwoods stand, And the road parts on either hand,

There came to him a sign.

King Guthrum was a war-chief,

A wise man in the field. And though he prospered well, and knew How Alfred's folk were sad and few, Not less with weighty care he drew

Long lines for pike and shield.

King Guthrum lay on the upper land,

On a single road at gaze, And his foe must come with lean array, Up the left arm of the cloven way.

To the meeting of the ways.

And lonfj ere the noise of armour,

An hour ere the break of light. The woods awoke with crash and cry. And the birds sprang clamouring harsh, and

high. And the rabbits ran like an elves' army

Ere Alfred came in sight.

The live wood came at Guthrum,

On foot and claw and wing, The nests were noisy overhead. For Alfred and the star of red.

BALLAD OF THE WHITE HORSE

All life went forth, and the forest fled Before the face of the Kinir.

But halted in the woodways

Christ's few were grim and grey, And each with a small, far, bird-like sight Saw the high folly of the fight; And though strange joys had grown in the night,

Despair grew with the day.

And when white dawn crawled through the wood,

Like cold foam of a flood. Then weakened every warrior's mood. In hope, though not in hardihood ; And each man sorrowed as he stood

In the fashion of his blood.

For the Saxon Franklin sorrowed For the things that had been fair,

For the dear dead women, crimson-clad,

And the great feasts and the friends he had ;

But the Celtic prince's soul was sad For the things that never were.

In the eyes Italian all things But a black laughter died; And Alfred flung his shield to earth And smote his breast and cried—

" I wronged a man to his slaying. And a woman to her shame.

And once I looked on a sworn maid That was wed to the Holy Name.

BALLAD OF THE WHITE HORSE

" And once I took my neighbour"'s wife, That was bound to an eastland man,

In the starkness of my evil youth, Before my griefs began.

" People, if you have any prayers.

Say prayers for me : And lay me under a Christian stone In that lost land I thought my own. To wait till the holy horn is blown.

And all poor men are free."

Then Eldred of the idle farm

Leaned on his ancient sword, As fell his heavy words and few; And his eyes were of such alien blue As gleams where the Northman saileth new

Into an unknown fiord.

" I was a fool and wasted ale—

My slaves found it sweet; I was a fool and wasted bread,

And the birds had bread to eat.

" The kings go up and the kings go down,

And who knows who shall rule; Next night a king may starve or sleep, But men and birds and beasts shall vveep At the burial of a fool.

" O, drunkards in my cellar,

Boys in my apple tree, The world grows stern and strange and new. And wise men shall govern you,

And you shall weep for me.

BALLAD OF THE WHITE HORSE

" But yoke me my own oxen,

Down to my own farm ; My own dog will whine for me, My own friends will bend the knee. And the foes I slew openly

Have never wished me harm.""

And all were moved a little,

But Golan stood apart, Having first pity, and after Hearing, like rat in rafter, That little worm of laughter

That eats the Irish heart. . .

And his grey-green eyes were cruel.

And the smile of his mouth waxed hard,

And he said, " And when did Britain Become your burying-yard ?

" Before the Roman lit the land, When schools and monks were none,

We reared such stones to the sun-god As might put out the sun.

" The tall trees of Britain

We worshipped and were vise, But you shall raid the whole land through And never a tree shall talk to you, Though every leaf is a tongue taught true And the forest is full of eyes.

" On one round hill to the seaward

The trees grow tall and grey.

And the trees talk together

When all men are away.

BALLAD OF THE WHITE HORSE

" O'er a few round hills forgotten The trees grow tall in rings,

And the trees talk together Of many pagan things,

" Yet I could lie and listen With a cross upon my clay.

And hear unhurt for ever

What the trees of Britain say."

A proud man was the Roman,

His speech a single one, But his eyes were like an eagle's eyes

That is staring at the sun. ,

" Dig for me where I die," he said,

" If first or last I fall-Dead on the fell at the first charge,

Or dead by Wantage wall;

" Lift not my head from bloody ground,

Bear not my body home, For all the earth is Roman earth
And I shall die in Rome."
Then Alfred, King of England,
Bade blow the horns of war. And fling the Golden Dragon out, With crackle and acclaim and shout,
Scrolled and aflame and far.
And under the Golden Dragon
Went Wessex all along, Past the sharp point of the cloven ways. Out from the black wood into the blaze
Of sun and steel and song.
And when they came to the open land They wheeled, deployed, and stood ;

BALLAD OF THE WHITE HORSE

Midmost were Marcus and the King, And Eldred on the right-hand wing. And leftwards Golan darkling, Li the last shade of the wood.
But the Earls of the Great Army
Lay like a long half moon, Ten poles before their palisades, With wide-winged helms and runic blades Red giants of an age of raids.
In the thornland of Ethandune.
Midmost the saddles rose and swayed,
And a stir of horses'" manes, Where Guthrum and a few rode high On horses seized in victory ; But Ogier went on foot to die,
In the old way of the Danes.

ETHANDUNE

Far to the King's right Elf the bard
Led on the western wing With songs and spells that change the blood ; And on the King"s left Harold stood,
The idnsman of the King.
Young Harold, coarse, with colours gay.
Smoking with oil and musk. And the pleasant violence of the young, Pushed through his people, giving tongue Foe wards, where, grey as cobwebs hung,
The banners of the Usk.
But as lie came before his line
A little space along, His beardless face broke into mirth. And he cried : " What broken bits of earth

BALLAD OF THE WHITE HORSE

Are here ? For what their clothes are worth I would sell them for a song."
For Colan was hung with raiment
Tattered like autumn leaves, And his men were all as thin as saints,
And all as poor as thieves.
No bows nor slings nor bolts they bore.
But bills and pikes ill-made; And none but Colan bore a sword,
And rusty was its blade.
And Colan""s eyes with mystery
And iron laughter stirred. And he spoke aloud, but lightly.
Not labouring to be heard.
" Oh, truly we be broken hearts,
For that cause, it is said. We liffht our candles to that Lord

That broke Himself for bread.
"But though we hold but bitterly
What land the Saxon leaves, Though Ireland be but a land of saints,
And Wales a land of thieves,
"I say you yet shall weary
Of the working of your word, That stricken spirits never strike,
Nor lean hands hold a sword.
"And if ever ye ride in Ireland,
The jest may yet be said. There is the land of broken hearts.
And the land of broken heads."

Not less barbarian laughter
Choked Harold like a flood, "And shall I fight with scarecrows
That am of Guthrum's blood?
"Meeting may be of war-men, Where the best war-man wins;
But all this carrion a man shoots Before the fight begins."
And stopping in his onward strides.
He snatched a bow in scorn From some mean slave, and bent it on Colan, whose doom grew dark; and shone Stars evil over Caerleon,
In the place where he was born.
For Colan had not bow nor sling,
On a lonely sword leaned he, Like Arthur on Excalibur
In the battle by the sea.
To his great gold ear-ring Harold Tugged back the feathered tail,
And swift had sprung the arrow. But swifter sprang the Gael.
Whirling the one sword round his head,
A gi'eat wheel in the sun. He sent it splendid through the sky, Flying before the shaft could fly— It smote Earl Harold over the eye,
And blood began to run.

BALLAD OF THE WHITE HORSE

Golan stood bare and weaponless,
Earl Harold, as in pain, Strove for a smile, put hand to head. Stumbled and suddenly fell dead; And the small white daisies all waxed red
With blood out of his brain.
And all at that marvel of the sword.
Cast like a stone to slay. Cried out. Said Alfred: "Who would see Signs, must give all things. Verily Man shall not taste of victory
Till he throws his sword away."
Then Alfred, prince of England,
And all the Christian earls, Unhooked their swords and held them up, Each offered to Colan, like a cup
Of chrysolite and pearls.
And the King said, "Do thou take my sword Who have done this deed of fire,
For this is the manner of Christian men.
Whether of steel or priestly pen,
That they cast their hearts out of their ken To get their hearts'" desire.
"And whether ye swear a hive of monks,

Or one fair wife to friend, This is the manner of Christian men,

That their oath endures the end.

" For Love, our Lord, at the end of the world.

Sits a red horse like a throne. With a brazen helm and an iron bow,

But one aiTow alone.

" Love with the shield of the Broken Heart Ever his bow doth bend,

BALLAD OF THE WHITE HORSE

With a single shaft for a single prize, And the ultimate bolt that parts and flies Comes with a thunder of split skies, And a sound of souls that rend.

*' So shall you earn a king's sword,

Who cast your sword away." And the King took, with a random eye, A rude axe from a hind hard by.

And turned him to the fray.

For the swords of the Earls of Daneland

Flamed round the fallen lord. The first blood woke the trumpet-tune, As in monk's rhyme or wizard's rune Beginneth the Battle of Ethandune

With the throwing of the sword.

BOOK VI

ETHANDUNE: THE SLAYING OF THE CHIEFS

A S the sea flooding the flat sands Flew on the sea-born horde, The two hosts shocked with dust and din, Ieft of the Latian paladin. Clanged all Prince Harold's howling kin On Colan and the sword.

Crashed in the midst on Marcus,

Ogier with Guthrum by. And westward of such central stir. Far to the right and faintlier,

BALLAD OF THE WHITE HORSE

The house of Elf the harp-player, Struck Eldred's with a cry.

The centre swat for weariness, Stemming the screaming horde,

And wearily went Colan's hands That swung King Alfred's sword.

But like a cloud of evening

To westward easily, Tall Eldred broke the sea of spears

As a tall ship breaks the sea.

His face like a sanguine sunset.

His shoulder a Wessex down. His hand like a windy hammer-stroke; Men could not count the crests he broke.

So fast the crests went down.

ETHANDUNE

As the tall white devil of the Plague

Moves out of Asian skies, With his foot on a waste of cities

And his head in a cloud of flies;

Or purple and peacock skies grow dark

With a moving locust-tower; Or tawny sand-winds tall and dry. Like hell's red banners beat and fly, When death comes out of Araby, Was Eldred in his hour.

But while he moved like a massacre He murmured as in sleep,

And his words were all of low hedges And little flelds and sheep.

BALLAD OF THE WHITE HORSE

Even as he strode like a pestilence, That strides from Rhine to Rome,

He thought how tall his beans might be If ever he went home.

Spoke some stiff piece of childish prayer,
Dull as the distant chimes, That thanked our God for good eating
And corn and quiet times—
Till on the helm of a high chief
Fell shatteringly his brand. And the helm broke and the bone broke
And the sword broke in his hand.
Then from the yelling Northmen Driven splintering on him ran
Fill] seven spears, and the seventh Was never made by man.
Seven spears, and the seventh
Was wrought as the faerie blades.
And given to Elf the minstrel By the monstrous water-maids ;
By them that dwell where luridly
Lost waters of the Rhine Move among roots of nations,
Being sunken for a sign.
Under all graves they murmur.
They murmur and rebel, Down to the buried kingdoms creep, And like a lost rain roar and weep
O'er the red heavens of hell.

BALLAD OF THE WHITE HORSE

Thrice drowned was Elf the minstrel,
And washed as dead on sand; And the third time men found him
The spear was in his hand.
Seven spears went about Eldred,
Like stays about a mast; But there was sorrow by the sea
For the driving of the last.
Six spears thrust upon Eldred
Were splintered while he laughed;
One spear thrust into Eldred, Three feet of blade and shaft.
And from the great heart grievously Came forth the shaft and blade,
And he stood with the face of a dead man. Stood a little, and swayed—
Then fell, as falls a battle-tower,
On smashed and struggling spears, Cast down from some unconquered town That, rushing earthward, carries down Loads of live men of all renown— Archers and engineers.
And a great clamour of Christian men
Went up in agony, Crying, " Fallen is the tower of VVessex
That stood beside the sea."
Centre and right the Wessex guard
Grew pale for doubt and fear. And the flank failed at the advance. For the death-light on the wizard lance-The star of the evil spear.
" Stand like an oak," cried Marcus,
" Stand like a Roman wall! Eldred the Good is fallen—
Are you too good to fall ?
" When we were wan and bloodless
He gave you ale enow ; The pirates deal with him as dung,
God ! are you bloodless now ? "
" Grip, Wulf and Gorlias, grip the ash !
Slaves, and I make you free ! Stamp, Hildred hard in English land. Stand Gurth, stand

Gorlias, Gawen stand ! Hold, Halfgar, with the other hand,
Halmer, hold up on knee!
" The lamps are dying in your homes,
The fruits upon your bough; Even now your old thatch smoulders, Gurth, Now is the judgment of the earth.
Now is the death-grip, now ! "
For thunder of the captain,
Not less the Wessex line. Leaned back and reeled a space to rear As Elf charged with the Rhine maids'" spear,
And roaring like the Rhine.
For the men were borne by the waving walls
Of woods and clouds that pass, By dizzy plain and drifting sea, And they mixed God with glamoury, God with the gods of the burning tree
And the wizard's tower and a-lass.
But Mark was come of the glittering towns
Where hot white details show, Where men can number and expound, And his faith grew in a hard ground Of doubt and reason and falsehood found. Where no faith else could grow.
Belief that grew of all beliefs One moment back was blown ;
And belief that stood on unbelief Stood up iron and alone.
The Wessex crescent backwards Crushed, as with bloody spear Went Elf roaring and routing, And Mark against Elf yet shouting. Shocked, in his mid-career.
Rio-ht on the Roman shield and sword Did spear of the Rhine maids run ;
But the shield shifted never,
The sword rang down to sever,
The great Rhine sang for ever. And the songs of Elf were done.
And a great thunder of Christian men
Went up against the sky, Saying, " God hath broken the evil spear
Ere the good man's blood was dry."
" Spears at the charge ! " yelled Mark amain.
" Death on the gods of death ! Over the thrones of doom and blood Goeth God that is a craftsman good, And gold and iron, earth and wood,
Loveth and laboureth.

BALLAD OF THE WHITE HORSE

" The fruits leap up in all your farms,
The lamps in each abode; God of all good things done on earth, All wheels or webs of any worth, The God that makes the roof, Gurth,
The God that makes the road.
" The God that heweth kino-s in oak
Writeth songs on vellum, God of gold and flaming glass, Confregit potentias Arcuum, scutum, Gorlias,
Gladium et bellum."
Steel and lightning broke about him.
Battle-bays and palm, All the sea-kings swayed among Woods of the Wessex arms upflung,
The trumpet of the Roman tongue, The thunder of the psahn.
And midmost of that rolling field
Ran Ogier ragingly, Lashing at Mark, who turned his blow, And brake the helm about his

brow,
And broke him to his knee.
Then Ogier heaved over his head
His huge round shield of proof;
But Mark set one foot on the shield,
One on some sundered rock upheeled,
And towered above the tossing field,
A statue on a roof.
Dealing far blows about the fight, Like thunder-bolts a-roam.

Like birds about the battle-field, While Ogier writhed under his shield Like a tortoise in his dome.

But hate in the buried Ogier
Was strong as pain in hell. With bare brute hand from the inside He burst the shield of brass and hide, And a death-stroke to the Roman's side
Sent suddenly and well.
Then the great statue on the shield Looked his last look around
With level and imperial eye;
And Mark, the man from Italy,
Fell in the sea of agony, And died without a sound.
And Ogier, leaping up alive,
Hurled his huge shield away Flying, as when a juggler flings
A whizzing plate in play.
And held two arms up rigidly.
And roared to all the Danes: " Fallen is Rome, yea, fallen
The city of the plains !
" Shall no man born remember,
That breaketh wood or weald. How long she stood on the roof of the world
As he stood on my shield.
"The new wild world forgetteth her
As foam fades on the sea, How long she stood with her foot on Man
As he with his foot on me.

" No more shall the brown men of the south
Move like the ants in lines, To quiet men with olives
Or madden men with vines.
" No more shall the white towns of the south,
Where Tiber and Nilus run, Sitting around a secret sea
Worship a secret sun.
" The blind gods roar for Rome fallen.
And forum and garland gone, For the ice of the north is broken.
And the sea of the north comes on.
" The blind gods roar and rave and dream
Of all cities under the sea, For the heart of the north is broken,
And the blood of the north is free.
" Down from the dome of the world we come,
Rivers on rivers down, Under us swirl the sects and hordes

And the high dooms we drown,
" Down from tlie dome of the world and down.

Struck flying as a skiff On a river in spate is spun and swirled Until we come to the end of the world

That breaks short, like a cliff.
" And when we come to the end of the world

For me, I count it fit To take the leap like a good river,

Shot shriekini£ over it.

BALLAD OF THE WHITE HORSE

" But whatso hap at the end of the world, Where Nothing is struck and sounds,

It is not, by Thor, these monkish men These humbled Wessex hounds—
" Not this pale line of Christian hinds,

This one white string of men, Shall keep us back from the end of the world.

And the things that happen then.
" It is not Alfred's dwarfish sword,

Nor Egbert's pigmy crown. Shall stay us now that descend in thunder. Rending the realms and the realms thereunder,

Down through the world and down."

There was that in the wild men back of him,

There was that in his own wild song, A dizzy throbbing, a drunkard smoke, That dazed to death all Wessex folk,

And swept their spears along.

Vainly the sword of Colan

And the axe of Alfred plied— The Danes poured in like a brainless plague,

And knew not when they died.

Prince Colan slew a score of them. And was stricken to his knee;

King Alfred slew a score and seven And was borne back on a tree.

BALLAD OF THE WHITE HORSE

Back to the black gate of the woods,

Back up the single way, Back by the place of the parting ways

Christ's knights were whirled away.

And when they came to the parting ways

Doom's heaviest hammer fell, For the King was beaten, blind, at bay, Down the right lane with his array, But Colan swept the other way,

Where he smote great strokes and fell.

The thorn-woods over Ethandune Stand sharp and thick as spears.

By night and furze and forest-harms

Far sundered were the friends in arms;

The loud lost blows, the last alarms, Came not to Alfred's ears.

The thorn-woods over Ethandune

Stand stiff as spikes in mail; As to the Haut King cr.me at morn Dead Roland on a doubtful horn, Seemed unto Alfred lightly borne

The last cry of the Gael.

BOOK VII ETHANDUNE: THE LAST CHARGE

A WAY in the waste of White Horse Dovn An idle child alone Played some small game through hours that

pass, And patiently would pluck the grass, Patiently push the stone.

On the lean, green edge for ever,
Where the blank chalk touched the turf,
The child played on, alone, divine,
As a child plays on the last line That sunders sand and surf.

For he dwelleth in high divisions
Too simple to understand, Seeing on what morn of mystery The Uncreated rent the sea
With roarings, from the land.

Through the long infant hours like days
He built one tower in vain— Piled up small stones to make a town. And evermore the stones fell down. And he piled them up again.

And crimson kings on battle-towers, And saints on Gothic spires.

And hermits on their peaks of snow. And heroes on their pyres,

And patriots riding royally,

That rush the rocking town. Stretch hands, and hunger and aspire. Seeking to mount where high and higher, The child whom Time can never tire.

Sings over White Horse Down.

And this was the might of Alfred,

At the ending of the way ; That of such smiters, wise or wild. He was least distant from the child.

Piling the stones all day.

For Eldred fought like a frank hunter
That killeth and goeth home ; And Mark had fought because all arms
Rang like the name of Rome.

And Colan fought with a double mind,

Moody and madly gay ; But Alfred fought as gravely

As a good child at play.

He saw wheels break and work run back

And all things as they were; And his heart was orbed like victory

And simple like despair.

Therefore is Mark forgotten,

That was wise with his tongue and brave; And the cairn over Colan crumbled.

And the cross on Eldred's grave.

Their great souls went on a wind away. And they have not tale or tomb ;

And Alfred born in Wantage Rules England till the doom.

Because in the forest of all fears Like a strange fresh gust from sea,

Struck him that ancient innocence That is more than mastery.

And as a child whose bricks fall down

Re-piles them o'er and o'er, Came ruin and the rain that burns. Returning as a wheel returns, And crouching in the furze and ferns He began his life once more.

He took his ivory horn unslung And smiled, but not in scorn:

" Endeth the Battle of Ethandune With the blowing: of a horn."

On a dark horse at the double way

He saw great Guthrum ride, Heard roar of brass and ring of steel, The laughter and the trumpet peal,

The pagan in his pride.

And Ogier's red and hated head

Moved in some talk or task ; But the men seemed scattered in the brier, And some of them had lit a fire,

And one had broached a cask.

And waggons one or two stood up,

Like tall ships in sight. As if an outpost were encamped

At the cloven ways for night.

And joyous of the sudden stay

Of Alfred's routed few, Sat one upon a stone to sigh, And some slipped up the road to fly, Till Alfred in the fern hard by

Set honi to mouth and blew.

And they all abode like statues—

One sitting on the stone, One half-way through the thorn hedge tall, One with a leg across a wall, And one looked backwards, very small.

Far up the road, alone.

Grey twilight and a yellow star

Hung over thorn and hill; Two spears and a cloven war-shield lay

Loose on the road as cast away, The horn died faint in the forests grey, And the fleeing men stood still.

" Brothers at arms," said Alfred,

" On this side lies the foe; Are slavery and starvation flowers,

That you should pluck them so ?

" For whether is it better

To be prodded with Danish poles, Having hewn a chamber in a ditch. And hounded like a howling witch. Or smoked to death in holes ?

" Or that before the red cock crow

All we, a thousand strong, Go down the dark road to God's house.

Singing a Wessex song ?

" To sweat a slave to a race of slaves,

To drink up infamy ? No, brothers, by your leave, I think Death is a better ale to drink. And by all the stars of Christ that sink,

The Danes shall drink with me.

" To grow old cowed in a conquered land. With the sun itself discrowned,

To see trees crouch and cattle slink —

Death is a better ale to drink,

And by high Death on the fell brink. That flagon shall go round.

" Though dead are all the paladins

Whom glory had in ken, Though all your thunder-sworded thanes

With proud hearts died among the Danes, While a man remains, great war remains : Now is a war of men.

" The men that tear the furrows,

The men that fell the trees, When all their lords be lost and dead The bondsmen of the earth shall tread

The tyrants of the seas.

"The wheel of the roaring stillness
Of all labours under the sun, Speed the wild work as well at least
As the whole world's work is done.
"Let Hildred hack the shield-wall
Clean as he hacks the hedge; Let Gurth the fowler stand as cool
As he stands on the chasm's edge;
"Let Gorlias ride the sea-kings
As Gorlias rides the sea, Then let all hell and Denmark drive, Yelling to all its fiends alive.

And not a rag care we."
When Alfred's word was ended
Stood firm that feeble line, Each in his place with club or spear, And fury deeper than deep fear,

And smiles as sour as brine.
And the King held up the horn and said,
"See ye my father's horn, That Egbert blew in his empery, Once, when he rode out commonly, Twice when he rode for venery,

And thrice on the battle-morn.

"But heavier fates have fallen
The horn of the Wessex kings, And I blew once, the riding sign, To call you to the fighting line And glory and all good things.

"And now two blasts, the hunting sign.
Because we turn to bay ; But I will not blow the three blasts.

Till we be lost or they.
"And now I blow the hunting sign. Charge some, by rule and rod;
But when I blow the battle sign, Charge all, and go to God."
Wild stared the Danes at the double ways Where they loitered, all at large,

As that dark line for the last time Doubled the knee to charge—
And caught their weapons clumsily.
And marvelled how and why— In such degree, by rule and rod. The people of the peace of God Went roaring down to die.

And when the last arrow
Was fitted and was flown, When the broken shield hung on the breast And the hopeless lance was laid in rest,

And the hopeless horn blown,

The King looked up, and what he saw
Was a great light like death. For Our Lady stood on the standards rent. As lonely and as innocent As when between white walls she went

And the lilies of Nazareth.
One instant in a still light
He saw Our Lady then. Her dress was soft as western sky. And she was a queen most womanly—

But she was a queen of men.
Over the iron forest
He saw Our Lady stand, Her eyes were sad withouten art, And seven swords were in her

heart—

But one was in her hand.

Tlicn the last rharge went blindly,

And all too lost for fear: The Danes closed round, a roaring ring, And twenty clubs rose o'er the King, Four Danes hewed at him, halloing, And Ogier of the Stone and Sling

Drove at him with a spear.

But the Danes were wild with lauirhter.

And the great spear swung wide, The point stuck to a straggling tree. And either host cried suddenly. As Alfred leapt aside.

Short time had shaggy Ogier

To pull his lance in line— He knew King Alfred's axe on high.

He heard it rushing through the sky,

BALLAD OF THE WHITE HORSE

He cowered beneath it with a cry

It split him to the spine : And Alfred sprang over him dead,

And blew the battle sign.

Then bursting all and blasting

Came Christendom like death, Kicked of such catapults of will, The staves shiver, the barrels spill. The waggons waver and crash and kill The waggoners beneath.

Barriers go backwards, banners rend. Great shields groan like a gong—

Horses like horns of nightmare Neigh horribly and long.

Horses ramp high and rock and boil

And break their golden reins, And slide on carnage clamorously, Down where the bitter blood doth lie, Where Ogier went on foot to die,

In the old way of the Danes.

" The high tide ! " King Alfred cried.

" The high tide and the turn! As a tide turns on the tall grey seas, See how they waver in the trees, How stray their spears, how knock their knees,

How wild their watchfires bum!

"The Mother of God goes over them.

Walking on wind and flame. And the storm-cloud drifts from city and dale,

BALLAD OF THE WHITE HORSE

And the White Horse stamps in the White

Horse Vale, And we all shall yet drink Christian ale In the village of our name.

" The Mother of God goes over them,

On dreadful cherubs borne; And the psalm is roaring above the rune, And the Cross goes over the sun and moon, Endeth the Battle of Ethandune

With the blowing of a horn."

For back indeed disorderly

The Danes went clamouring. Too worn to take anew the tale, Or dazed with insolence and ale. Or stunned of heaven, or stricken pale

Before the face of the Kine;,

For dire was Alfred in his hour

The pale scribe witnesseth, More mighty in defeat was he Than all men else in victory, And behind, his men came murderously,

Dry-throated, drinking death.

And Edgar of the Golden Ship

He slew with his own hand, Took Ludwig from his lady's bower, And smote down Harmar in his hour, And vain and lonely stood the tower—

The tower in Guelderland.

And Torr out of his tiny boat. Whose eyes beheld the Nile, Wulf with his war-cry on his lips.

And Hacro born in the eclipse,

Who blocked the Seine with battleships

Round Paris on the Isle. ^

And Hacon of the Harvest-Song, And Dirck from the Elbe he slew.

And Cnut that melted Durham bell.

And Fulk and fiery Oscar fell,

And Goderic and Sigael, And Uriel of the Yew.

And highest sang the slaughter.

And fastest fell the slain. When from the wood-road's blackening throat A crowning and crashing wonder smote

The rear-guard of the Dane.

For the dregs of Colan's company—

Lost down the other road— Had gathered and grown and heard the din, And with wild yells came pouring in, Naked as their old British kin,

And bright with blood for woad.

And bare and bloody and aloft

They bore before their band The body of their mighty lord, Colan of Caerleon and its horde, That bore King Alfred's battle-sword

Broken in his left hand.

And a strange music went with him.

Loud and yet strangely far; The wild pipes of the western land,

Too keen for the ear to understand, Sang high and deathly on each hand When the dead man went to war.

Blocked between ghost and buccaneer, Brave men have dropped and died ; And the wild sea-lords well might quail As the ghastly war-pipes of the Gael Called to the horns of White Horse Vale, And all the horns replied.

And Hildred the poor hedger

Cut down four captains dead. And Halmer laid three others low. And the great earls wavered to and fro For the living and the dead.

And Gorlias grasped the great flag,

The Raven of Odin, torn ; And the eyes of Guthrum altered.

For the first time since morn.

As a turn of the wheel of tempest

Tilts up the whole sky tall, And cliffs of wan cloud luminous Lean out like great walls over us,

As if the heavens might fall.

As such a tall and tilted sky

Sends certain snow or light. So did the eyes of Guthrum change, And the turn was more certain and more strange

Than a thousand men in flig-ht.

BALLAD OF THE WHITE HORSE

For not till the floor of the skies is split, And hell-fire shines through the sea,

Or the stars look up through the rent earth's knees,

Cometh such rending of certainties,

As when one wise man truly sees What is more wise than he.

He set his horse in the battle-breach

Even Guthrum of the Dane, And as ever had fallen fell his brand, A falling tower o'er many a land. But Gurth the fowler laid one hand Upon this bridle rein.

King Guthrum was a great lord.

And higher than his gods-

He put the popes to laughter, He chid tlie saints with rods,

He took this hollow world of ours For a cup to hold his wine;

In the parting of the wood ways There came to him a sign.

In Wessex in the forest.

In the breaking of the spears,

We set a sign on Guthrum To blaze a thousand years.

Where the high saddles jostle

And the horse-tails toss, There rose to the birds flying A roar of dead and dying; In deafness and strong crying

We signed him with the cross.

Far out to the winding river The blood ran down for days,

When we put the cross on Guthrum In the parting of the ways.

BOOK VIll

THE SCOURING OF THE HORSE

TN the years of the peace of Wessex,

When the good King sat at home; Years following on that bloody boon When she that stands above the moon Stood above death at Ethandune And saw his kingdom come—

When the pagan people of the sea Fled to their palisades,

Nailed there with javelins to cling,

BALLAD OF THE WHITE HORSE

And wonder smote the pirate king, And brought him to his christening And the end of all his raids.

(For not till the night's blue slate is wiped

Of its last star utterly, And fierce new signs writ there to read, Shall eyes with such amazement heed, As when a great man knows indeed

A greater thing than he.)

And there came to his chrism-loosing

Lords of all lands afar, And a line was drawn north-westerly That set King Egbert's empire free, Giving all lands by the northern sea

To the sons of the northern star.

In the days of the rest of Alfred, When all these things were done,

And Wessex lay in a patch of peace, Like a dog in a patch of sun—

The King sat in his orchard, Among apples green and red.

With the little book in his bosom And the sunshine on his head.

And he gathered the songs of simple men That swing with helm and hod,

And the alms he gave as a Christian

Like a river alive with fishes ran;
And he made gifts to a beggar man As to a wandering god.

And he gat good laws of the ancient kings,
Like treasure out of the tombs; And many a thief in thorny nook, Or noble in sea-stained turret shook. For the opening of his iron book,
And the gathering of the dooms.

Then men would come from the ends of the earth,
Whom the King sat welcoming. And men would go to the ends of the earth
Because of the word of the King.

For folk came in to Alfred's face
Whose javelins had been hurled On monsters that make boil the sea, Crakens and coils of mystery.

Or thi'ust ill ancient snows that be The white hair of the world.

And some had knocked at the northern sates
Of the ultimate icy floor, Where the fish freeze and the foam turns black, And the wide world narrows to a track, And the other sea at the world's back
Cries through a closed door.

And men went forth from Alfred's face,
Even great gift-bearing lords.
Not to Rome only, but more bold.
Out to the high hot courts of old,
Of negroes clad in cloth of gold,
Silence, and crooked swords,

Scrawled screens and secret gardens
And insect-laden skies— Where fiery plains stretch on and on To the purple country of Prester John
And the walls of Paradise.

And he knew the might of the Terre Majeure,
Where kings began to reign; Where in a night-rout, without name, Of gloomy Goths and Gauls there came White, above candles all aflame,
Like a vision, Charlemagne.

And men, seeing such embassies, Spake with the King and said: *' The steel that sang so sweet a tune On Ashdown and on Ethandune,

Why hangs it scabbarded so soon, All heavily like lead?
" Why dwell the Danes in North England,
And up to the river ride? Three more such marches like thine own Would end them; and the Pict should own Our sway; and our feet climb the throne
In the mountains of Strathclyde,""

And Alfred in the orchard,
Among apples green and red, With the little book in his bosom,
Looked at green leaves and said:
" When all philosophies shall fail,
This word alone shall fit; That a sage feels too small for life.

And a fool too larje for it.
BALLAD OF THE WHITE HORSE
" Asia and all imperial plains
Are too little for a fool; But for one man whose eyes can see, The little island of Athelney
Is too large a land to rule.
" Haply it had been better
When I built my fortress there,
Out in the reedy waters wide,
I had stood on my mud wall and cried:
' Take England all, from tide to tide— Be Athelney my share
" Those madmen of the throne-scramble-
Oppressors and oppressed— Had lined the banks by Athelney,
THE SCOURING OF THE HORSE
And waved and wailed unceasingly, Where the river turned to the broad sea, By an island of the blest.
" An island like a little book
Full of a hundred tales, Like the gilt page the good monks pen, That is all smaller than a wren, Yet hath high towns, meteors, and men,
And suns and spouting whales;
" A land having a light on it
In the river dark and fast. An isle with utter clearness lit. Because a saint had stood in it; Where flowers are flowers indeed and fit,
And trees are trees at last.
BALLAD OF THE WHITE HORSE
" So were the island of a saint;
But I am a connnon king, And I will make my fences tough From Wantage Town to Plymoutli Bluff, Because I am not wise enough
To rule so small a thing."
And it fell in the days of Alfred,
In the days of his repose. That as old customs in his sight AVere a straight road and a steady light, He bade them keep the White Horse white
As the first plume of the snows.
And right to the red torchlight. From the trouble of morning grey.
They stripped the White Horse of the grass As they strip it to this day.
THE SCOURING OF THE HORSE
And under the red torchlight
He went dreaming as though dull,
Of his old companions slain like kings,
And the rich irrevocable things
Of a heart that hath not openings. But is shut fast, beins full.
And the torchlight touched the pale hair
Where silver clouded gold, And the frame of his face was made of cords. And a young lord turned among the lords
And said : " The King is old."
And even as he said it A post ran in amain, Crying : " Arm, Lord King, the hamlets arm.
BALLAD OF THE WHITE HORSE
In the horror and the shade of harm, They have burnt Brand of Aynger's farm— The

Danes are come again!
"Danes drive the white East Angles
In six fights on the plains, Danes waste the world about the Thames,
Danes to the eastward—Danes!"
And as he stumbled on one knee.
The thanes broke out in ire, Crying: "Ill the watchmen watch, and ill
The sheriffs keep the shire."
But the young earl said: "Ill the saints.
The saints of England, guard The land wherein we pledge them gold; The dykes decay, the King grows old.
And surely this is hard,
"That we be never quit of them;
That when his head is hoar He cannot say to them he smote, And spared with a hand hard at the throat,
'Go, and return no more.'"
Then Alfred smiled. And the smile of him
Was like the sun for power. But he only pointed: bade them heed Those peasants of the Berkshire breed, Who plucked the old Horse of the weed
As they pluck it to this hour.
"Will ye part with the weeds for ever?
Or show daisies to the door? Or will you bid the bold grass
Go, and return no more?

BALLAD OF THE WHITE HORSE

"So ceaseless and so secret
Thrive terror and theft set free;
Treason and shame shall come to pass
While one weed flowers in a morass;
And like the stillness of stiff grass The stillness of tyranny.

"Over our white souls also
Wild heresies and high Wave prouder than the plumes of grass,
And sadder than their sigh.

"And I go riding against the raid,
And ye know not where I am; But ye shall know in a day or year, When one green star of grass grows here; Chaos has charged you, charger and spear,
Battle-axe and battering-ram.

THE SCOURING OF THE HORSE

"And though skies alter and empires melt,
This word shall still be true: If we would have the horse of old,
Scour ye the horse anew.

"One time I followed a dancing star
That seemed to sing and nod, And ring upon earth all evil's knell; But now I wot if ye scour not well Red rust shall grow on God's great bell
And grass in the streets of God.""
Ceased Alfred; and above his head The grand green domes, the Downs,
Showed the first legions of the press,
Marching in haste and bitterness For Christ's sake and the crown's.

BALLAD OF THE WHITE HORSE

Beyond the cavern of Colan,
Past Eldred"'s by the sea,
Rose men that owned King Alfred's rod,
From the windy wastes of Exe untrod,
Or where the thorn of the grave of God
Burns over Glastonbury,

Far northward and far westward
The distant tribes drew nigh.
Plains beyond plains, fell beyond fell,
That a man at sunset sees so well.
And the tiny coloured towns that dwell
In the corners of the sky.

But dark and thick as thronged the host.
With drum and torch and blade,
The still-eyed King sat pondering.

THE SCOURING OF THE HORSE

As one that watches a live thing,
The scoured chalk ; and he said,
" Though I give this land to Our Lady,
That helped me in Athelney,
Thoush lordlier trees and lustier sod
And happier hills hath no flesh trod
Than the garden of the Mother of God
Between Thames side and the sea,

" I know that weeds shall grow in it
Faster than men can burn ;
And though they scatter now and go,
In some far century, sad and slow,
I have a vision, and I know
The heathen shall return.

BALLAD OF THE WHITE HORSE

" They shall not come with warships,
They shall not waste with brands,
But books be all their eating,
And ink be on their hands.

" Not with the humour of hunters
Or savage skill in war,
But ordering all things with dead words,
Strings shall they make of beasts and birds,
And wheels of wind and star.

" They shall come mild as monkish clerks,
With many a scroll and pen;
And backward shall ye turn and gaze,
Desiring one of Alfred's days.
When pagans still were men.

THE SCOURING OF THE HORSE

" The dear sun dwarfed of dreadful suns,
Like fiercer flowers on stalk,
Earth lost and little like a pea
In high heaven's towering forestry,
—These be the small weeds ye shall see
Crawl, covering the chalk.

" But though they bridge St. Mary's sea,
Or steal St. Michaers wing—
Though they rear marvels over us,
Greater than great Vergilius
Wrought for the Roman king ;

" By this sign you shall know them,
The breaking of the sword.
And Man no more a free knight,
That loves or hates his lord.

BALLAD OF THE WHITE HORSE

" Yea, this shall be the sign of them,
The sign of the dying fire;
And Man made like a half-wit,
That knows not of his sire.

" What though they come with scroll and pen,

And grave as a shaven clerk, By this sign you shall know them,
That they ruin and make dark ;
" By all men bond to Nothing,
Being slaves without a lord. By one blind idiot world obeyed.
Too blind to be abhorred ;
"By terror and the cruel tales
Of curse in bone and kin. By weird and weakness winning,

THE SCOURING OF THE HORSE

Accursed from the beginning, By detail of the sinning, And denial of the sin ;
" By thought a crawling ruin,
By life a leaping mire. By a broken heart in the breast of the world.
And the end of the world's desire;
" By God and man dishonoured,
By death and life made vain, Know ye the old barbarian.
The barbarian come again—
" When is great talk of trend and tide,
And wisdom and destiny. Hail that undying heathen
That is sadder than the sea.

BALLAD OF THE WHITE HORSE

" In what wise men shall smite him,
Or the Cross stand up again, Or charity or chivalry, My vision saith not; and I see No more; but now ride doubtfully
To the battle of the plain."
And the grass-edge of the great down
Was cut clean as a lawn. While the levies thronged from near and far. From the warm woods of the western star, And the King went out to his last war
On a tall grey horse at dawn.
And news of his far-off fighting
Came slow and brokenly From the land of the East Saxons,
From the sunrise and the sea,

THE SCOURING OF THE HORSE

From the plains of the white sunrise,
And sad St. Edmund's crown, Where the pools of Essex pale and gleam
Out beyond London Town
In mighty and doubtful fragments,
Like faint or fabled wars. Climbed the old hills of his renown. Where the bald brow of White Horse Down
Is close to the cold stars.
But away in the eastern places
The wind of death walked high, And a raid was driven athwart the raid, The sky reddened and the smoke swayed. And the tall grey horse went by.

BALLAD OF THE WHITE HORSE

The gates of the great river
Were breached as with a barge, The walls sank crowded, say the scribes, And high towers populous with tribes
Seemed leaning from the charge.
Smoke like rebellious heavens rolled Curled over coloured flames,

Mirrored in monstrous purple dreams In the mighty pools of Thames.

Loud was the war on London wall,

And loud in London gates, And loud the sea-kings in the cloud Broke through their dreaming gods, and loud

Cried on their dreadful Fates.

THE SCOURING OF THE HORSE

And all the while on AVhite Horse Hill

The horse lay long and wan, The turf crawled and the fungus crept, And the little sorrel, while all men slept,

Unwrought the work of man.

With velvet finger, velvet foot.

The fierce soft mosses then Crept on the large white commonweal All folk had striven to strip and peel. And the grass, like a great green witch's wheel.

Unwound the toils of men.

And clover and silent thistle throve,

And buds burst silently, With little care for the Thames Valley

Or what things there might be

BALLAD OF THE WHITE HORSE

That away on the widening river,

In the eastern plains for crown Stood up in the pale purple sky One tun-et of smoke like ivory; And the smoke changed and the wind went by,

THE END

Printed in the USA
CPSIA information can be obtained
at www.ICGtesting.com
CBHW081121081224
18657CB00026B/610